CONTENTS

Part One: Farm Boy	5
Pool	6
Parents	9
Aloneness	13
Part Two: No Longer Alone	16
Dorothy (Dot)	17
Part Two: No Longer Alone	20
Urine Bath	21
The Unlucky Duo	25
Controlling Dot	28
Story Time	31
Transformations	35
Can You Hear Me Now?	39
Twice a Hero	42
Sweet Sweet Freedoms	45
Part Three: Times of Change	47
Long Explains	48

Dot Gets Glad	50
Philosophically Speaking	53
A Little Sexy Time	56
Back to the Mission	60
Part Four: One-Step Forward : Two Steppin Back	62
Technicals and Jellie	63
The Show Online	66
Dot's Attempt to Hurt a Man	70
A Little Bit of Damage	74
Abe's Attempt to Hurt a Woman	76
Self Tests	80
Funny Tampons	83
Part Five: Start of End	85
DGAF	86
Worldly Belongings and ByeByes	87
The Cow	90
Next Moves	92
Motel Chances	95
Part Six: Finished	97
Rude Awakening	98
A Boy and His Cow	102
A note from the dark mind of Sea Caummisar	104

THE LIGHT AND THE STICK: EXTREME HORROR

The Light and the Stick: Extreme Horror

From the dark mind of Sea Caummisar

THE LIGHT AND THE STICK: EXTREME HORROR

Copyright © 2024 by Sea Caummisar

All rights reserved. No portion of this book may be reproduced in any form without permission from the publisher, except as permitted by U.S. copyright law. For permissions contact sharoncheatham81@gmail.com

This is entirely a work of fiction, pulled out of my own imagination. All characters and events are not real (fictitious). If there are any similarities to real persons, living or dead, it is purely coincidental.

This has never happened in real life. This is not about any person's life. It's false. Fiction; lies that authors (like myself) write on paper to entertain people.

If this has ever happened to you, I apologize. I swear that these are characters that I dreamt up in my sleep.

Lights are not necessarily bad. Sticks with nails in them are not necessarily bad. It just happens for this book title I chose that part of the image to focus on. Maybe the way they're used in this book is bad. MAYBE

Also, being mean is not nice. Be kind to each other.

WARNING

YOU! Yes, you. The one reading these words.

Your mental health is important to me.

If you have triggers, put this book down.

Do not read any further.

If you feel the need to continue reading, and you feel mentally distressed, do me and you both a favor. STOP READING.

If it's about the money you spent on the book, return it. Get a refund.

Because your mental health is more important to me than money.

PART ONE: FARM BOY

POOL

What was once a galvanized horse trough was now repurposed into a swimming pool of sorts.

Nostalgia from Abe's childhood was his inspiration.

As a kid, hot summer days on the farm, spent feeding animals and mucking stalls, were rewarded with an evening swim in a small trough similar to the one he was filling at this very moment.

Ten years ago, he didn't even have the good sense to wash the sweat from his body, nor scrape the feces from beneath his fingernails before jumping into the murky water of the two feet deep, two feet wide, and six foot long container.

Back then, it felt so small.

Now it felt so large.

Technically, it held one hundred and seventy gallons of liquid, but that was only if you filled it to the brim.

Abe had read somewhere that the average adult human urinated one hundred and eighty gallons a year. That was approximately a half gallon per day.

It hadn't taken him six months to fill his new pool

halfway full of his own piss.

His reasoning was that fact was due to the beer he drank, his kidneys working overtime, and his body cleansing itself of more fluid daily than the average human. It stood to reason that if he consumed more liquid than the average person, he would also produce more.

And when it came to beer, he consumed plenty of it. More than his fair share.

The worst part of relieving his kidneys in the trough was the long walk from the modest house on the farm, to the backside of the property. So more often than not, Abe spent his evenings outside, drinking his beer and enjoying nature.

Looking at the moon. Counting the stars. Throwing rocks into a nearby pond. Shooting at squirrels and birds that dared to climb on a tree in the woodsy area, that filled the edges of his land with beauty.

The fields were now mostly overgrown, with only patches that were still fruitful.

The majority of the animals were gone, too, but a few were still around to serve Abe's purposes.

It was covered above the trough, a makeshift wooden roof, a place he selected purposely to keep the rainwater from mixing with his pool of piss.

That did not prevent insects from either climbing into or flying above the liquid, some falling to their death to drown in the bodily waste. It made Abe laugh when he saw a fly struggling to swim, its wings too moist to flap, its body weighed down and not able to produce flight.

Instead of its tracheae taking in oxygen, the insect was deprived of the life substance, replaced with human urine, struggling to its eventual death and succumbing to the amber colored and acidic fluid.

At this very moment, the stream flowing from his dick into the trough was warm, and he wondered what the temperature of the pool was.

It was a nice autumn day. The type of weather where the days were hot, mornings and evening pleasant, and the nights just a tad chilly.

Abe had learned to ignore the smell of his piss pool.

It was nothing compared to a childhood of shoveling feces (horse, pig, and cow). Odors were a thing people could get used to, some even using the term nose blindness to refer to an aroma that should bother them but didn't.

Abe emptied his bladder, feeling relieved from the pressure of four beers passing through his kidneys, and zipped up his pants.

Curiosity of temperature got the better of him, and Abe stuck the tips of three fingers into the fluid.

Just as he suspected.

His newest urine floating on the top was much warmer than the fluid that had been left below it to fester for months.

PARENTS

It was at the age of seventeen, about four years ago, that Abe lost his parents.

Actually, 'lost' is a word that Abe hated.

They weren't lost.

They were gone, in a sense.

There was a difference between the two.

His love for beer was something his mother used to say was a curse, one she feared he would inherit from his father.

The one good thing Abe could say about his father was that the man was a hard worker.

Tending the farm was no easy task, and the reason why Abe had to start helping out at a young age.

Twenty acres (rotated between corn, wheat, and soybean) didn't plant, grow, tend or harvest itself. Two horses, six cows (for milk), and pigs set up on a slaughtering/ auction rotation needed to be cared for and fed.

Abe's dad did this job, and he did it with a bottle of whiskey in his hand, dependent on the help of his wife and son. It kept the family's stomachs full of food and a roof over their heads. But not much more, except supplying his father's drinking habit.

Abe's mother spent her time cleaning up vomit and icing her own bruises (usually shaped as her husband's fists) when she wasn't busy helping with milking the cows.

The smell of his own pool of urine, Abe could get used to.

The animal droppings he shoveled, even that wasn't bad in his opinion.

However…

The smell of his parents was something that still bothered him.

Their bodies were kept in a cylindrical structure. Not that there was much other use for the silo due to the fields not having many plants.

What used to be a holding place for their yearly crops, equipped with fans to remove humidity and keep the moisture content controlled, was now a grave for both Abe's mother's and father's rotting corpses.

Abe always visited them at night, when it was too dark to see how much they had decomposed. In the beginning, when they were newly dead, Abe had to sometimes fight rats and other small animals from feeding upon their flesh.

Now, years later, he suspected they were more bone than anything.

The fans helped with the smell, a force of wind lifting and clearing the putrid aroma from the structure, but it still lingered like a cloud. A bad omen of what we all turn into. Lifeless bodies and a stench that stained even the strongest noses, like a scar permanently etched onto Abe's sense of smell.

His parents were not lost.

He stood mere feet from them, often, to pay his respects.

There had been no family to come around looking for them.

Not even any friends that visited.

Occasionally, the small-town shop owner would ask about them, and Abe had to buy beer and whiskey to keep up the ploy that his father was still living. Always spoke of how busy they were with the farm, and how they were getting older, and now the chore of running into town was Abe's responsibility.

Abe never reported their deaths.

And he didn't have one particular reason as to why he neglected to do so.

Fear.

Pride.

Sadness.

Shame.

Regret.

Remorse.

Guilt.

Too many emotions and reasons to blame just a single one.

If he never spoke of their death, then maybe it never happened.

If nobody else knew, then it was his secret and only his, and maybe that meant it only existed in his reality. Maybe in another reality, their deaths had never occurred.

What good could come from telling anyone?

Abe did well to plant enough crops to feed himself. The cows gave him milk. Pork was often on the menu due to a supply of breeding pigs.

And all cash (mostly made from selling pigs) was spent on sundries and alcohol.

The tax bill (for the property) had come and gone, and Abe wasn't sure how he'd pay it this year.

The one thing Abe did right was graduating from high school a few years ago, right before his parents' death. It made him feel like he'd done something right with his life.

After all, he was still young and staring at his dead parents' outlines in the shadow of night was a reminder that even though their lives had ended, his was just beginning.

ALONENESS

Before going to bed, Abe stopped by the barn to say goodnight to Dottie.

Her udders drooped, a confirmation of her age, and her cylindrical teats hung too low. The pustules that had formed grew larger every day, an invasion of dark lumps that formed at the base, invaded fresh areas of skin every day.

Dottie had been around ever since he lost his parents and had become a friend to him.

When there was no other physical interaction available from a living person, Dottie was always there for him.

The way her soft teats brought comfort to his hands when he milked her was something he had learned to rely upon for physical comfort.

The cow was a great listener, and would even tilt her head at times to acknowledge her understanding of his words.

The boil-like growths had also affected her milking abilities.

In the beginning, there wasn't much change in the dairy she produced, but now pus floated in the fluid like the tiny pearl balls of tapioca pudding.

Abe wasn't sure if it was harmful for him to ingest, so to be sure, he would always pluck them out before drinking, discarding the odorous pockets like they were poison.

Abe spoke to her, and she looked at him. "In a few days, things around here will change. I just have to figure out what to do with you."

He knew that she understood him, and wished for her to speak to him.

But she didn't even moo.

His father had been known to get drunk and do what Abe considered to be unspeakable with some of the animals, Dottie in particular.

Abe was at the age when he longed for physical touch and sexual relief.

Erections still popped up frequently for no good reason, but never had he violated Dottie in the ways he'd witnessed his father.

The way his dad would stand behind the cow, his pants around his ankles, both of his wrinkled hands grasped on either side of her hips/rump area, humping and groaning and moaning.

Dottie would turn her head, the same way as when Abe spoke to her, but didn't put up a fuss about it.

Abe had masturbated in front of the cow, just to see if she watched him.

An experiment of sorts to see if she was interested, but she rarely moved her head to the side, not even when he stroked the shaft of his cock feverishly like a pubescent teen.

Not even when his hot semen erupted like a spouting water fountain, collecting on the hay on the barn floor, did she moo.

Dottie wasn't interested.

But she was when he spoke.

"I still have time to think about what I'll do with you, but I really feel like this is something I must do. You can understand that, right?"

Dottie's head didn't turn, but her large eyes blinked suddenly, slowly, and purposely.

"I knew you'd understand. This is for the best. We won't be lonely for long."

PART TWO: NO LONGER ALONE

DOROTHY (DOT)

The first time he'd seen her all those years ago at school, Abe knew that he loved her. Even her name was comforting and reminded him of his father's favorite cow. Dorothy was assigned to her at birth, but people rarely called her by that name.

Dot was what everyone knew her as.

And Abe loved the sound of it.

It matched the small-button nose that was perfectly centered on her symmetrical face. Her hazel eyes shone as bright as lightning strikes among dark storm clouds.

And she smelled delicious.

Having lived on the farm his entire life, Abe wasn't accustomed to people smelling like food, and Dot's strawberry scented shampoo and candy apple body lotion made his nose happy.

The only other female he had ever spent time around (his mother) worked with them in the fields and the barns, and never once had he known her to smell as pretty as Dot.

Opposed to his clothing, hers were always clean

and new.

Her shoes never had holes in them.

When she smiled at him that first time, Abe could feel his heart trying to beat out of his chest. It was almost like time stopped him in a trance and all he could do was stare.

A few years ago felt like a lifetime since they'd first met, but ever since that day, she'd stolen his attention and his love.

The contrasts between the two of them that made him fall for her, made her equally like him back.

The slight bulge of his farm-earned biceps caught her eye, and she even thought it was cute how he got tongue-tied when he tried to speak to her.

Her father was a president of a bank, and none of his co-workers' sons had calluses on their hands from a hard day's work. Those boys, when she tried dating them, weren't as nice as Abe, and they only tried to get her naked and use her body.

Abe was genuinely kind to her and asked how she felt, and about her thoughts and her dreams.

The farm boy saw her as more than just someone to try and have sex with.

It was a short-lived romance, her parents not approving of her dating a boy from a lower income family, especially one a few years ahead of her in school.

Shortly after their newly formed romance had ended, Abe graduated from high school, and didn't see Dot on a daily basis in the classrooms or hallways.

Shortly after that, he lost his parents, and Abe found himself outside Dot's window late one night, renewing their spark for one another, her frequently sneaking out to spend time with him enjoying sweet talks under the moon.

The disapproval from her parents of dating him made it hard for them to see each other, and their restricted time spent together put a damper on their relationship.

Dot had recently graduated from high school, and days after turned eighteen, a legal adult.

That didn't prevent her parents from enforcing their choices on her, insisting that she go to college to further her education.

Unbeknownst to her parents, Dot spent a day on the farm with Abe, and realized that his lower lifestyle wasn't becoming to her. She was accustomed to having spare money, new clothing, store-bought food, and all the other qualities of life that came with having parents with a small amount of wealth.

Dot told her parents that she agreed to go to college, and once again upon their insistence, they choose a university several states away, which would essentially sever her ties to Abe.

Abe was not happy with her decision and cried large tears down his cheeks when she told him goodbye.

PART TWO: NO LONGER ALONE

URINE BATH

"Smile for the camera!" Abe yelled.

There was a stripe of black electrical tape wound tight, forcing Dot's wrists together; and two other black strips, one across her ankles and the other at her knees.

"It's a shame to cover that pretty mouth of yours," Abe whispered in her ear, "But it's necessary. I guess it's funny that I told you to smile for the camera when you have that pretty silver tape across your lips."

Dot's body shook in the sandy dirt, her trying her best to flail her limbs free from her bindings.

"That's right," Abe encouraged her movements. "Show them how you're fighting for your freedom. I bet they'll really love that!"

Abe turned off the camera and slung Dot over his shoulder like a fireman carrying someone out of a burning home. His voice was now calm, other than a slight quiver of fear.

"Ten hours drive, well round trip, to go get you from college and bring you back. You know how much I love you? I wouldn't be doing this if I didn't love you so much."

Dot couldn't reply, but Abe was accustomed to speaking to people who didn't respond. His parents in particular.

With care, he carefully placed her nude body beside the horse trough, and went back for the camera.

Abe watched her wiggle in the tall blades of glass, similar to a worm, just much larger.

It took him a few minutes, but soon he had arranged the tripod in the distance, mounted the camera on top, and framed the piss pool in the center of the digital screen.

"And action!" Abe screamed.

Her bare flesh, warm from the sun, felt good in his hands that were slid into the crevice where her arms met the trunk of her body. It was easy lifting her, even with her dainty frame struggling to break free from him.

With a splash, he flung her into the metal container, acrid urine overflowing from the brim of the makeshift pool.

Purposely, her hands had been bound together in front of her, allowing Dot the chance to extend her arms and rise her head above the fluid.

The way her knees had also been bound together made it impossible for her to climb out.

Abe stood behind the camera, watching the love of his life trying to fight for oxygen through the small screen. The urge to look away hit him, but he knew he had to watch. Just in case he had to step in and save her.

Dot sounded like a pig sucking air through her nostrils, and her bloodshot eyes spoke to him. Aged-urine had burned the mucous membranes of her sight organs.

Her long, blonde hair, thick and luxurious, was now sopping wet and matted to her head like a melted helmet.

Still, Abe knew this had to be done, even if it hurt his heart to witness her struggling.

Seconds turned into minutes, and once Dot had positioned herself so that the upper half of her body was hanging over the rim, Abe stopped the camera and lifted her, not bothered that he was now also covered in his own bodily waste.

"Shhh," Abe whispered. "It'll be okay. Let's get you cleaned up."

Abe wasted no time carrying her back inside.

After he laid her in the bathtub, Dot's eyes widened as he pulled a folding knife from his pocket, and cut away the electrical tape from around her wrists.

"Your hands are free now," he told her, "and by the time you remove the tape from your legs, you'll be locked in this bathroom. Trust me, it's for the best. Take a good bath. Clean yourself up."

True to his word, he stepped out of the small room, closing the wooden door behind him, and secured a hinged hasp that he slid a thick lock through.

Before stepping away, Abe leaned against the door. "Trust me, this is for the best."

Dot must have also removed the tape across her

mouth, because after taking a few steps, he heard her call out for him, by name.

Abe kept walking.

THE UNLUCKY DUO

There was only one bathroom, so Abe didn't have the opportunity to wash the stale piss from his clothing. The smell didn't bother him.

There were other matters that were more important than being clean.

Time was of the essence, and he had things that needed to be done.

Abe held a wallet up to a dim light and looked through its contents. "Twenty bucks? No credit cards? But a driver license. I see your name is Jeff. Just above the age of twenty. So sad. So young."

The man struggled, his wrists and legs taped up in the same fashion as Dot's were, but his limbs were attached to a chair. Groans and moans came from his mouth, a dirty red bandana tied around his head tightly, covering his mouth, soaking up some of the blood that drained from his broken nose.

"I'll get to questions later. Or maybe I can answer some of them now." Abe spoke calmly, his words precise and collected. Next he picked up a purse, unzipped it, and removed another wallet, a female version much larger than the male counterpart's bifold. "Jennifer. Same age. No cash. But a credit card. And what a beauty you are."

The woman was also taped to a chair, the side of her face bruised, her left eye swollen and bruised so hard that she could barely see out of it.

Abe spoke directly to her now. "You look so much like Dot that it's uncanny. Other than your hair being darker and longer. Same pale skin. Eyes the exact color. Even her slim build."

Jeff clenched his fists and fought so hard that he shook the chair to which he was tied, raising one of the legs from the dirt floor.

Abe wasn't bothered. "Like I said, I'll explain. No need to get upset. It's too late for that. What's done is done, and this is my way of bettering my life. Are you two in love? I suppose so, the way I saw the pair of you cuddled in that tent. Someone should have told you that it's not smart to camp so far away from civilization.

"Jennifer, can I call you Jen? I've watched you for a while now. You've done nothing wrong, other than looking like the woman I love. And Jeff, you wouldn't even be here if you hadn't chased after me in those woods. I only wanted her, but you had to be a hero. Maybe I wasn't quiet enough when I approached her, her panties down around her ankles, peeing behind that tree.

"A macho man. You tried to save her. You're lucky I

didn't have to shoot you. Guns are overrated, but at close range also work well as blunt weapons.

"I'm a man, driven by love. Motivated. Will-powered by it."

Abe ended his little speech, all the while emptying Jennifer's purse, sorting through a variety of lipsticks and compact mirrors and ink pens.

"Abe!"

After hearing his name called, Abe looked behind him, towards the other side of the small home. "That's her. Dot. And I love her so much. Would do anything for her, and I guess it's time that I prove it."

Turning his back on his two prisoners, Abe walked, long strides, to reach his destination quickly. "I'm coming, love. Everything is fine. No need to yell. I promise I'll take care of everything. You don't need to worry about a thing."

Jeff and Jen looked at each other, tears streaming down her cheeks, each water drop forming to the curve of the left side of her swollen face, leaving behind a salty trail.

CONTROLLING DOT

Unlocking and opening the bathroom door, Abe held the pistol in his hand, but didn't dare point it directly at Dot.

Wrapped in a towel, her shoulders still glistening with bath water, Dot shook her head. "You don't need that thing, Abe. Listen to me. Put it down."

"No."

Stepping forward, the towel fell from her body, and for just a moment Abe's eyes lingered on her nude female form.

"Baby," Dot continued to move forward, hoping to entice him. "This is me. You really don't need that thing."

The way she pronounced the words 'that thing', like what she was referring to was evil and poisonous, Abe became very aware of the gun in his hand. "Stop!" he screamed, stepping away from her. "No! They're in there waiting. They can probably hear us. I'm in control here, so no!"

Dot flinched with each loud sound he made towards her and covered her face with her hands.

"Don't you even dare think about raising a hand towards me. I'll shoot you if I have to!" Abe's warning was loud and menacing. "Why can't you understand? I love you so much."

The girl, now practically cowered away from him, cleared her throat and attempted to de-escalate the situation. "Abe, you're scaring me-"

"Good! You should be afraid. Very afraid! Put on the bathrobe! Right now! Cover yourself and shut up!"

++++++++++

Abe marched Dot into the room with his two other prisoners, the gun pointed towards her back.

"It's so dark in here," Dot remarked as she stepped over some empty, discarded beer cans. "Who are they? Why are there two people in here taped to chairs?"

"Shut up!" Abe yelled, losing his patience. "There's a method to my madness. Can't you be quiet for just a few minutes and let me think?"

"You're not thinking this through," she argued. "You really should listen to me."

"No! I have thought this through! Sit down!" he yelled, motioning his gun towards another chair. "Sit down and shut up!"

Obediently, Dot did as instructed and sat, ensuring her robe stayed closed over her bare chest.

Abe reached over to a table and threw two sets

of handcuffs towards her. "Put these on. Each wrist and then the arm of the chair."

"No! I won't do this, Abe."

It only took two footfalls to close the gap between him and her, and due to the proximity of the weapon, Dot snapped the silver bracelets around her wrists and the chair arms.

"That wasn't hard, was it?" Abe asked. "If you stay quiet, I won't tape your mouth shut. But one peep out of you, and I'll gag you, same as I did them." Abe once again motioned with the pistol, this time towards Jeff and Jen, who craned their necks as much as they could out of harm's way, just in case their captor decided to pull the trigger.

"Good. Are we all comfy now?" Abe asked. "I'll be right back."

Abe walked out of the room, a man with a mission, soon to return.

Dot's handcuffs clinked against the chair arms. "I should've fought harder. Why'd I listen to him?"

Jeff and Jen both looked at her, and it wasn't until this moment that Dot realized how badly their faces were bloodied and bruised. They made noises through their gagged lips, but no words could be deciphered.

"He's done gone and lost his damn mind," Dot said, like it was some sort of revelation, more to herself than the couple. "Why is he acting like an idiot?"

STORY TIME

Dot begged for her freedom. "Abe, let me out of these handcuffs now."

Abe placed a single finger over his puckered lips. "Shh. This picture here," Abe held it up for his three captive audience members to see, "this is my Ma. This picture was used to scare me as a child."

The picture was faded, a torn corner with another rolled and peeling apart.

Abe stood and got closer to show each person a better view of the photo, and had to shove it really close to Jennifer's one good non-swollen eye for her to see it.

The photograph was of a woman, just as Abe had said, but her face had been scratched out, removed, showing nothing but her body that could have been attached to any head. Above her head, the female body held a wooden stick in her left hand, a single nail hammered into the side of the opposite end. Behind her was a door with two lightbulbs lit above it, highlighting with a perfect amount of illumination that single nail.

"This was what my mother used when she

whipped me as a kid. That wooden stick. Dad, drunk one night, nailed that nail to it, in hopes that when she'd spank me, it'd tear my skin right open. So I pretty much behaved. That picture was showed to me when I started acting up, to put the fear of God in me or something-"

"Abe," Dot interrupted. "You've never told me any of this. Why would you keep something like that a secret from me? Why would you reveal something so personal to these strangers? Is this why you're acting like this?"

Abe raised his index finger to his puckered lips again. "Shhh. Do I need to gag you, too?"

After looking at the picture, Abe set it aside and reached for a bottle of whiskey. "My Ma, she never spanked me hard, and rarely ever with anything but her hand. Never once did she snag me with that nail. It was just her way..." His words lingered in the air like a storm cloud brewing in the sky as he fought back tears from forming in his eyes.

"Her way of what?" Dot asked, her words so quiet they were practically whispered.

"It was her way of saving me. Protecting me from my Father. If I didn't mind her, he'd be ten times harder on me, punching me with closed fists and all, the same as he did her. It took her teaching me fear, and it took me many years to learn that it was to make me, and my life, better."

Swiping at his eyes to hide his crying, and taking a chug from the small glass bottle, Abe turned his back to his audience.

Seemingly, out of nowhere, Abe produced that wooden stick from a table hidden in a darkened corner.

Dot squinted and leaned forward. "Is that the same stick?"

Abe nodded, and held it closer for her to see, more in the lighted center of the room.

"Is that mud? What's all over it? Is that rust on the nail?" Dot asked.

"It's blood," Abe replied, mindlessly running his finger up and down the skinny shaft of the nail.

"Is it yours?" Dot asked.

"No!" Abe lashed out. "And what'd I tell you about speaking? Shut up!"

In a fury, Abe raised the bottle to his lips and turned it upwards, in such a quick gesture that he couldn't get the liquored liquid into his body fast enough.

"Why are you doing this?" Dot asked. "I don't understand. Just uncuff me. I hate seeing you so upset. This isn't-"

Abe threw the now empty glass pint across the room, it shattered upon impact as it struck the wall. Large shards of glass laid in a heap on the dirt floor.

Without another word, he pulled another bandana from his back pocket, and Abe folded it lengthwise until it was the perfect shape to tie around Dot's head.

She fought as hard as she could, wiggling her head as much as she could to evade him, and continually screamed. "No! Abe! No! Abe!"

He was persistent, and once he slid the cloth between her upper and lower rows of teeth, he tied it around the backside of her head, securing it tightly.

Even that didn't make Dot be quiet, but at least he couldn't make out what she was saying. It merely sounded like background noise until he tired of even those sounds coming from her and slapped a thick piece of tape over her mouth.

TRANSFORMATIONS

"I really hate doing this," Abe told Dot as he stood behind her. "I have to do what I have to do. And that's all there is to it."

Her ears perked up as she heard a buzzing sound coming from behind her. Dot turned around to see what it was only to realize he was holding an electronic hair trimmer, compact, its metal teeth sliding across each other, generating that creepy sound.

Abe didn't even bother removing the bandana that was tied around her head because his intention was to shave the top of her head first, and in a rush before he lost his gumption.

Dot wiggled the lower half of her chin and used her tongue to lick against the backside of the tape until her mouth was only covered by the bandana.

So badly, she wanted to shake her head to deter Abe, but knew that would make shaving her head even worse.

"NNNNNN! AAAAAAAAAA!"

"Please Dot!" Abe cried out, his shaking hand trying his best to shave away straight strips of hair along the top dome of her skull. "Don't make this harder than it has to be."

The bandana in her mouth not only collected particles of saliva that her vocal cords were forcing upwards of her throat, but it also absorbed the tears, genuine and real, falling down her face.

"You'll still be beautiful after this," Abe said, surety in his voice.

From where the cloth was still tied around the back of her head, the long hair that had been removed at the root fell to the side of her head, no longer attached, but more tangled in her gag.

Due to the thickness of Dot's hair, it took several swipes to give her cranium that buzzed, short and stubby, effect of an almost shaved head.

Abe attended to her with care, keeping a steady hand, not putting the blades too close to her skin unless he was confident he wouldn't nick her tender flesh.

Through her tears, Dot stared at the camera, her eyes begging for help to whomever may ever see this recorded footage.

Abe even did the backside of her head, above the cloth, and when finished with that, he untied the bandana, and made sure to get all the hair on her head. "See, that's not so bad, is it?" he asked.

Dot couldn't answer, and instead she sat in the chair, shaking and crying. "Why?" Why? Why?" she repeated.

"It's okay. You're still beautiful," he assured her.

+++

Abe wasn't as kind to Jen.

His movements with the humming razor were not gentle. Whether he nicked the flesh beneath her hair didn't bother him in the least.

It didn't help that she kept turning her head, twisting her neck, and moaning through her mouth gag.

"This is your fault," Abe warned her. "You're making this harder than it has to be."

She'd tilt her head to the side to eek away from the shaver, but it'd only test Abe's patience, forcing him to press harder and follow her movements. Once, the razor nicked the top of her ear, which immediately leaked a trail of blood down her neck.

Jeff fought harder against his restraints, the chair creaking beneath his weight. Trying his best to protect his girlfriend from the madman. "Ssstttphphph."

"It's just hair," Abe replied calmly. "This has to be done."

Long strands of hair fell away from her scalp, tiny slivers cracked open, bleeding slightly the least of her worries. It was illogical and confusing as to why he'd want her bald.

After removing all of Jen's hair, Abe smiled, and turned his head back and forth between both women. "You two look even more alike now."

CAN YOU HEAR ME NOW?

Jen's chair was centered in front of the camera, a red light flashing above the tripod mount to signify that it was recording. Abe zoomed in so that Jeff nor Dot could be seen on the tiny digital screen.

"Perfect," Abe observed, using both thumbs and index fingers to form a square in the distance. "You look so much like Dot, especially with your head buzzed, that it's ridiculous."

Jen's lips quivered around the moist bandana in her mouth. Tears kept falling and the bruised lump on the side of her face seemed to swell even more around her eye.

"I guess I got lucky that you're wearing nothing but an oversized men's t-shirt. Suppose it was great when going out to the woods to piss, but even greater that it could be something that Dot could easily wear too. Everything has to be perfect. What's the word?" Abe snapped his fingers. "Consistent. I have to be consistent."

Dot refused to be quiet, constantly doing her best to communicate with Abe.

"Sound won't matter much," he said. "I'll add my own."

The three tied up people looked to each other for answers, but nothing made sense.

++++

Now masked, only Abe's beady eyes visible through the balaclava, when he spoke, his words were garbled. "This will hurt, but you'll live."

Getting closer to Jen, one hand behind his back like he was hiding what he was holding, was enough inspiration for Jeff and Jen to struggle harder against their restraints.

"We start small," Abe said aloud, but mostly to himself.

When Abe revealed what he was holding, a handheld pair of pruning shears, she cried even louder, an uncontrollable sob, which turned into hyperventilating.

The tool was worn, the rubber covering the handles smeared and stained. The metal blades, corroded from age, and filthy in color, were very menacing.

Squeezing the item, Abe made the shears open and close, creating a snapping sound.

"It's just an ear," Abe said soothingly, his way of

consoling the woman who looked so much like the love of his life. "Thin. Fragile. Easy to snip."

Ignoring the ear that was already slightly cut open by the razor, Abe set his sights on the uninjured ear, while a frantic Jen cried out through her gag and did her best to get away from the sharp pruning tool.

Her attempts were fruitless, and when the metal blades came together, a crunching sound filled the air as the upper half of her ear was severed, forever separated from her body.

The blood was thin, but the gush was solid and thick, spurting upwards, until it lessened into a trickle.

Seeing Jen injured gave Jeff the strength he needed to try and be her hero.

TWICE A HERO

"Stop this!"

Jeff's clear words pulled Abe from his trance of watching his victim squirm and scream, him even noting that it was comical the way Jen was flopping her head around as if she was trying to outrun her pain.

"What?" Abe asked aloud.

"I said leave her alone!"

Abe turned his head to see that Jeff had chewed his way through his gag, like a mouse on a mission, which now allowed him to speak.

Jeff's muscles bulged, his arms trying their best to snap the thick tape.

His chair creaked beneath him, the screws that attached the arms of the chair now loose.

Wiggling his hips, Jeff used his body weight to aid in his escape.

It was inevitable. The chair would soon give, which would also free the angry Jeff.

Abe had to think fast, but he wasn't quick enough. Still holding the hand-sized pruning tool, he waved it out in front of him, in hopes it would deter Jeff from trying to rush into him.

One chair leg snapped, forcing Jeff to the ground, his legs quick to react and stand, his adrenaline giving him super strength.

The chair legs were still taped to his shins, and the chair arms to his wrists, but Jeff could now move about. Driven by fury, Jeff made his way to Abe, not caring the man held a sharp object in his hand.

Dot and Jen both cried out through their gags, their sounds not quite excitement but not fearful either. More like spectators, forced to only watch and not participate.

Both hands out in front of him, Jeff used the taped on wooden chair arm to his advantage as a weapon.

Jeff jumped on top of Abe, knocking his captor off his feet, forcing the wood across the downed Abe's throat, depriving him of the ability to breathe.

Abe tried to fight, but Jeff had the upper hand, pinning Abe's body to the dirt floor.

Jeff smashed the wooden chair arm into Abe's face multiple times, ripping the flesh open, the backside of Abe's head pounding against the ground with each attack.

Abe stopped moving, stopped trying to fight back, his neck limp, his head curled into his shoulder.

"Wahoo!" Jeff cheered, up righting himself and began un-taping the wooden chair parts from his body. "Hang on baby. I'm coming."

Jeff made his way towards Jen, freeing her mouth first and next her limbs, and then wrapped his arms around his girl to comfort her. "It's okay now. It's all okay."

"You did it!" Jen exclaimed, not taking her eyes off Abe. "Is he dead? Did you kill him?"

"I don't know," Jeff answered earnestly, pulling himself away from his lover's embrace. "You unite her, and I'll check on him."

With trembling legs and shaking hands, Jen made her way to Dot, and started to free her.

"He's not dead," Jeff announced. "Unconscious but not dead."

SWEET SWEET FREEDOMS

Jeff was still bent over Abe's body, two fingers pressed against his neck and feeling a pulse. "Has anyone seen a phone? We need to call the cops."

"I doubt Abe has one," Dot replied calmly. "I haven't seen our cells either," Dot said, standing up and stretching her legs. "I'll start looking for them, though."

Jen went to her boyfriend's side. "Should we tie him up or something?"

"Look here!" Dot said with pride. "Look what I found!"

"Is it our phones?" Jen asked innocently. "Call the police. 9-1-1 right now, please!"

"Oh," Dot turned to face the others, something held in her hand. "It's not our phones. It's the gun."

Jeff stood suddenly, alert and giving his full attention, one hand held out in front of him. "Give me that. I can use it in case he wakes up."

Dot waved it towards them, the weapon loosely in

her palm.

Jen shrieked out of the way. "Be careful with that! You could seriously hurt one of us if it accidentally fired!"

"Like this?" Dot asked.

Dot placed the grip against her palm and threaded her pointer finger around the trigger, and squeezed.

Jeff, who had been only a few feet away, fell down, his leg bent and him holding his thigh against his upper body. "You shot me! You shot me!"

The wound of his knee was a large hole, painted crimson, fresh blood flowing onto the dirt floor.

"Look what you did!" Jen yelled, bending down to attend to her lover's injury. "He's fainting! Jeff, stay with me," she begged, lightly slapping him against his cheek.

"Is that exposed bone in your leg?" Dot asked. "The white stuff under the blood. Look how the flesh is broken, so fragile. Meat flapping loosely, showing us what we're really made of."

"Are you nuts? We need to find the phone and call him an ambulance!"

"Nu-uh," Dot responded and clicked her tongue. "Nope. You need to shut up before I blow your head off."

It was that moment that Jen displayed fear in her eyes, glassy and squinting in disbelief.

"Yeah, back away from Abe. Right now. Or I'll kill you dead where you are." Dot's threat wasn't hollow.

PART THREE: TIMES OF CHANGE

LONG EXPLAINS

"Abe! Abe! Wake up!" Dot screamed, not lowering the weapon, which was still pointed towards Jen.

When Abe didn't respond, Dot kicked him. "Get up you idiot! I need your help!"

Jen held both hands out in front of her, a weak attempt to possibly shield herself from a bullet if Dot pulled the trigger again. "Why are you doing this? You were tied up, too! You couldn't have been in on this!"

"What's happening?" Abe asked, trying to sit up, rubbing his eyes. "What is happening?"

"You dropped the ball is what's happening!" Dot yelled furiously. "You had some nerve tying me up! You're lucky she freed me. Otherwise, they'd have called the police!"

"Sorry," Abe said, reaching out for the gun.

"Sorry? That's all you can say?" Dot wasn't in the mood for nonsense. "That's it? I guess we can fully acknowledge your stupidity now!"

Abe shrugged, not caring that Dot wouldn't give him the gun.

"Why'd you tie me up? I thought we were a team?"

"We are a team. That was my way of protecting you from having to do some of the hard stuff. Stuff that you shouldn't have to do. Like the murder part or the torture part."

"I like those parts!"

Jen interrupted. "Wait a minute! You are in on this together? Will someone ever explain this? Because it's not making much sense to me."

"It's simple. My parents tried to keep Abe and me apart by sending me away to college. I love Abe, even if he can be stupid from time to time…"

"Hold up!" Abe objected.

"I do love him, but he's poor. I love money, too. So Abe kidnaps me, sends video footage to my dad, and gets ransom money. So we can run away together and be rich. Except, that's where you come in. You look like me. Abe would never hurt me. So he was going to hurt you."

"And see, I tried to make it easy on you! I don't want you involved with this," Abe argued. "I'm the man. I should be doing it all."

"Just a few more questions," Jen said with a raised hand like she was a child in a classroom. "Why'd you kidnap Jeff, too? Why'd you shave her head if I'm supposed to be playing her on film? Why'd you-"

"Enough!" Dot screamed. "We've already established that Abe isn't very smart. That's enough questions. C'mon, Abe, help me tie them back up."

DOT GETS GLAD

"So you wanted to protect me?" Dot asked. "That's your excuse for tying me up? Even though you failed. First by bringing Jeff here, and second by letting him break loose."

"Sorry, honey," Abe hung his head. "I'm so sorry. I just know you wanted that money so bad. I've gotten some great videos to send your folks. I need a bit more, and do some edits, then we can send it to them with a ransom letter."

"*I'm sorry, honey,*" Dot mocked, cocking her head left and right and speaking in a high-pitched voice. "What are you? A sissy? Cause I'm sure not a sissy."

"I'm not a sissy," Abe replied meekly.

Dot didn't want to give up possession of the gun, but she sure did enjoy bossing Abe around. "Tie him up, nice and good, on the kitchen table. Get her back in that chair so we can get back to recording later."

++++++

Jeff laid on the table, vulnerable, large strips of tape weaved around his body, attaching him securely to the table.

"Shooting him was boring," Dot confessed. "It was over too quick. I didn't really even get a chance to see it."

Abe shrugged, not sure what she wanted to hear. From past experience, he had learned it was fine to just agree with her. So he nodded.

Now that she was examining the injury up close, Dot's mouth hung open, her fingers eager to explore.

"Reminds me of when you let me help you slaughter that hog," Dot said, casually, her fingers now sticky with Jeff's blood. "The way that pig hung upside down, the way its head unhinged when I slit its throat. The way the blood drained from his body. Except Jeff's blood isn't as much."

Abe shrugged, not sure how the two things, pigs and Jeff, were similar, but nodded anyway.

Using one hand to widen the wound, Dot plunged her fingers of her other hand deeper, pinching thumb and index finger together. "This feels like some kind of tight chord. Like a guitar string or something."

She didn't ask, but Abe knew it was her way. "That's probably a tendon, if I had to guess. I can't see it from here, but chances are."

Dot continued feeling around inside the wound. "His knee cap is shattered. Isn't it supposed to be one large bone? His isn't. The bullet did that, I suppose. Still, it was boring."

"I don't want you bored, honey," Abe offered genuinely. "This is the start of our lives together. I want it to be memorable."

"Okay then. Can we have some fun before we get back to recording?"

"Absolutely, honey."

PHILOSOPHICALLY SPEAKING

Abe was more concentrating on the fact that he was sharing the same space as Dot, the woman he had worked hard to keep in his life, and not bothered with her actions.

"Is this the same as with animals?"

"What?" Abe hadn't heard the full question. "How do you mean?"

"Did you feel bad when you hurt animals? Should I feel bad when I hurt him?"

"Why do you want to hurt him? I grew up on a farm. I was raised to snap a chicken's neck, or bleed a hog, for food. Or for profit. To feed others. Why would I feel bad about that?"

"So does that mean I shouldn't feel bad for wanting to hurt Jeff?"

"I didn't want to hurt Jen. I was only doing it to get good video footage to get money from your folks. I was doing it to better my life, your life. Our lives."

"But I want to. For no good reason. Just because he's here and I can."

Abe shrugged. "If it makes you happy…"

Jeff was now half conscious, his face covered in sweat, his eyes open, but staring blankly off into space.

Dot was watching him closely. "Like this."

Her feminine hands were small in comparison to Jeff's bony fingers, but she wrapped them around his pinky, and pulled it sideways, away from his palm.

Crack.

"Look! He practically jumped. Well, flinched as best he could, being taped up like a worm on the table." Dot was proud of her accomplishment, now bent over, her face inches from his broken digit. "What is that? Would you say a ninety-degree angle? Permanent damage? A finger should never bend that far."

Abe shrugged. "I didn't want to bring him here. It's just that I had to do something with him because he tried to stop me from taking Jen."

"I'm glad he's here."

"Shouldn't we be working on the video? The sooner we get it made, the sooner we can try and get money from your dad, and the sooner we can get away from here. Go anywhere that you want."

"I suppose so. But aren't you tempted? You know we have to kill him and her, both of them. They cannot live after this." The same hand she used to break Jeff's finger was the very same one that she was using to rub on Abe's chest. "Hurting him makes me tingly. Inside. In my private area. The spot you love so much. Just like when I watch horror movies, and get scared, and I get aroused."

"Murder and torture are two very different things, I don't mind killing for our reason, but making them suffer-"

"Gets me hot and bothered!"

A LITTLE SEXY TIME

Eyes on Abe, and one hand on his chest, Dot got closer to Jeff's hand that was taped to the edge of the table.

The pinky, bone broken somewhere around the knuckle closest to his palm, and a ligament overstretched and torn, quivered slightly, Jeff fading in and out of consciousness.

But her attention was on Abe. And Dot was rubbing her bare vagina gently against the broken finger, causing Jeff to moan consistently.

Abe couldn't resist his woman, not when she was nude and horny, not when she was rubbing his chest and licking his neck. Her tongue caressed that special spot he enjoyed so much (directly below his ear).

Abe didn't even notice that the lower half of her body was grinding the corner of the table, using Jeff's broken nub as some sort of sex toy.

"Abe, I want you," she whispered, voice full of

seduction. "I want you to screw me so bad."

Her boyfriend couldn't undo his pants fast enough, his erection sprung against the zipper, waiting to be released.

To free his bulging penis, Abe had to step back, and that's when he noticed Jeff's pinky finger wedged between Dot's plump, external vaginal lips.

"What are you doing?"

"Making the best of this situation." It wasn't what she said, it was how she said it, in a sultry whisper. "Don't you wish your dick was his finger? Or maybe even your tongue."

Abe had never been shy in terms of tasting his lover's natural juices, and dropped to his knees, hoping she'd pull away from the nearly unconscious man's hand.

Once he dropped to his knees, Dot angled her body so that more of Jeff's finger disappeared into what he assumed was inside her.

"Taste it! Taste me! Taste his pain!" she cried out,

"Dot. Hold up. Are you oka-"

"Fine! Fuck me from behind while I suck his finger, imagining it being your cock in my face!"

Abe was conflicted, but the blood filling his penis won, and slid himself into her tight cavity doggy style, while she sucked on Jeff's broken finger.

Her sucking turned into chewing, which broke Jeff's flesh, causing a seepage of blood, filling the cracks of her teeth and tainting her taste buds. "Harder!" she cried out.

And Abe thrust harder.

Jeff groaned, the sounds coming through his gagged mouth, teasing her to moan louder.

Dot raised up, pulling on Jeff's shirt, working it around the tape until his bare nipple was exposed.

The moment she sank her teeth into the tiny bud, severing the nipple from Jeff's body, was the exact time that Abe looked up to see why she was wiggling.

Her hand was behind Jeff's leg, slightly resting on the table under the knee cap that had taken the bullet.

With a cupped palm, and a single finger, Dot was fingering the backside of his leg, where the bullet exited his body, her finger pumping furiously, rising shattered bones out from beneath the fractured flesh.

The trail of blood running down the man's chest, the bone being forced from his open wound, and the fact that his girlfriend was more interested in the unconscious man didn't phase Abe in the least.

It did occur to him though that he hadn't even noticed that the bullet hole went in one side and out the other (through and through) until he was balls deep in his girl. This did strike him as an odd observation, but it didn't deter him from the current task at hand.

Abe thrust one last time, unable to contain his orgasm any longer, hot liquid filling her moist cavity.

Dot moaned with pleasure, a sound Abe had never heard her make before.

It felt good knowing that he could please the woman that he loved; so Abe grinned. Teeth and all.

Then fell forward, collapsing on his bent over lover, from exhaustion.

BACK TO THE MISSION

"I have enough footage," Abe declared, sitting in front of his computer. "The video will start with the photo of my mom holding the stick, and then I'll chop up you swimming in the urine trough, shaving your head, cutting off that piece of her ear. The sequence will be so fast that anything will be hard to decipher."

"How'd you learn to do all of this? I never knew you were this smart," Dot said as she pecked him on the cheek with puckered lips. "Not bad for a farm boy."

Abe shrugged. "I don't know. I just enjoy using the computer and making videos for the music I like. I got bored a lot, and self-taught myself how to do this. It's not like it's hard."

"How will we get it to my parents?"

"I'm thinking email. With a warning that if they go to the police, you're dead. Do you think they'll suspect me? If I make this about money, they won't think it's for love, right?"

"Not sure. Record my voice, me asking dad for the money. Let that play over your video. If I beg, that'll get to him bad. He'll want to save me. I'll even give hints that I was taken from the college campus and how afraid I am being so far away from home. They'll never think it's you that way."

"Good idea," Abe started punching keys on his keyboard.

"That stuff about your parents, earlier. When you told Jen and Jeff about your parents. Was that true? You'd never told me that stuff before."

"Yeah, it was all true, but not the full truth."

"Meaning? Does that have something to do with why your parents abandoned you a few years ago."

It took Abe a moment to remember that he had told Dot that his parents moved away, leaving him the farm. "Something like that. Can this discussion wait until after we get this video done?"

"You both are really sick, aren't you?" Jen screamed in the background.

"Why isn't she gagged?" Abe asked.

"Listen, Jeff is hurt. I'm hurt. But nobody is dead yet. It's not too late to let us go. If it's money you want, we can get it for you. From my parents. Or Jeff's parents." Jen was speaking from a place of fear. "It's not too late. We can move past this."

"Gag her," Abe said. "I need to get to work on this video."

PART FOUR: ONE-STEP FORWARD : TWO STEPPIN BACK

TECHNICALS AND JELLIE

After gagging Jen, Dot sat down by the computer. "How do you know they can't trace the email?"

"I'm using a VPN, which is basically a fake web address for this computer. And I'm sending the email from a platform known for its anonymity. Used a burner phone for the verification. Fake names and-"

"Where'd you learn all of this?"

"You know that web show I watch? That show I told you about. Called 'My Vagina Smells Like Sulfur'. It's dark web stuff. You can learn a lot of stuff in the chats and in searches. And they want people to send in videos, and there's a tutorial on how to do it anonymously."

Dot scratched her chin. "You have mentioned it, but I've never seen the show. Can we watch one?"

Abe shrugged. "Sure. I need some beer anyway. Perfect timing for a break."

++++++

After some typing, and guzzling a beer, Abe turned the computer monitor so that Dot could get a clear view of the screen.

"Welcome back, my loyal followers!" a tinny came through the computer's built-in speakers. "I am Madame Midnite and am thrilled that you're here."

The screen was doing the opposite of fading to black. Instead, it started as a black screen that gradually got brighter, centering in the frame a nude woman sprawled across a settee.

"Click the link below for the full details, but this next segment is home viewers and where we showcase their talents. Oh, this is the kind of stuff that gets me juicy." The woman's fingers disappeared into the folds of her vagina.

Abe clicked the pause symbol, and started explaining. "See this link right here? When you click it, it teaches you how to do stuff online without getting caught."

Dot's mouth hung open. "What?"

Abe sat a little higher, proud that he was smart enough to learn information from the internet to help them get money from her dad. "Yeah, I've been studying up. I really think we can pull this off."

"That woman is naked! Is she fingering herself! Everything about her is so fake! Her lips, her tits, even her hair! I can't see her backside, but I bet that's fake too! Do you think she's pretty?"

Abe opened his mouth, gulped in some air, and swallowed so hard that his Adam's apple bobbed. "You're missing the point. I'm showing you how I've learned to do all of this."

"Yeah, but you didn't tell me that you're looking at naked women online!"

Abe shrugged.

"Do you want to have sex with that woman?"

"With Madam Midnite? That would be like wanting to have sex with a movie star. That's ridiculous. It could never happen!"

"But what if she did come here? What if she did want to have sex with you?"

Abe bit his tongue and shrugged, once again. "You're the only one I want. Haven't I proven that to you by doing this? We're trying to get some cash together so we can run away together and live our lives together."

"You also gagged me and tied me up."

"I did that to protect you from all of this! I didn't want you to have to do any of this! And what about you with Jeff? He's half dead, and you practically fingered yourself with his limp hand!"

Dot reached over and hit the mouser, clicking the play button. "Let's see what's next on this show. I bet it's porn! It better not be porn!"

"I haven't seen this episode. It may or may not be porn. It's just home viewers sending in video. How am I supposed to know what it is?"

THE SHOW ONLINE

The high quality image of Madam Midnite faded to black, and a grainier picture that was obviously far from high definition took its place.

It was a side view of a woman lying on a bed, her hands above her head and belted to bed posts. The scene was so dark that it almost looked like it lacked color and was filmed in black and white.

"See! It's a naked woman! On a bed! Are you trying to tell me that this isn't porn?" Dot's question was voiced in an accusatory tone.

Abe shrugged.

A man came into the shot, only his torso and lower extremities showing, wearing nothing but a white t-shirt (no pants).

His legs were chunky, his thighs rubbing together as he climbed onto the bed. The man that wasn't showing his face on camera squatted above the woman, his ball sack resting on the woman's chin, her mouth sucking on a ball gag.

It was quiet. Too quiet.

Until the man farted, which caused Abe to laugh.

Following the noisy air expelled from his rump, a steady stream of semi-liquid and semi-solid substance poured from his anus, coating the woman's face with his excrement.

The woman closed her eyes, shook her head from side-to-side, and even tried to fling her restrained body the best that she could to get away from the situation.

But it was fruitless.

The man laughed, as did Abe.

The woman started heaving, her neck convulsing as her body tried to upchuck from a flat position with something stuck in her face hole.

Immediately, with no ending and no warning, the scene changed.

To a view from a shaky camera, presumably from someone trying to hold it while they recorded.

There was a woman, a black hood covering her face, her tits spilling over the top of a desk that her hands were nailed into. The silver heads of both nails barely showed due to being punctured thoroughly through the backsides of her hands, but the leaking blood trailing down the sides of her flesh made it look real.

Dot covered her gaping open mouth with a hand and stared in silence.

Whoever was holding the camera revealed thick stubby, hairy fingers, dirt beneath his fingernails.

Using a pair of needle nose pliers, he poked at the

woman's long fingernails, painted pink with some type of shimmer to the color, until one of the opened prongs slid beneath her fingernail, lifting it from her body.

The manly hand snapped the grip together, closing the metal clamps fiercely.

Then he pulled towards him. Away from her. Inevitably forcing the thin fingernail free from her body.

A slimy sliver of blood tethered the removed portion to the tip of her finger, until it burst, dissipating like a popped bubble.

The video cut away again, to a new scene. This one, a close up of a mouth, the lips spread by a cheek retractor, showing perfectly white and straight teeth.

This was probably the best picture in terms of the recording being quality.

The light was bright. The picture was steady. The teeth were perfectly centered in the frame.

Gloved hands came into view, one holding a chisel, the other a hammer.

The chisel was placed against the gum line of the top two teeth, and then the hammer swung swiftly, pounding the metal deep into the mouth.

The gum broke, blood pouring, almost blocking the view of the two chipped away teeth that now rested on the victim's tongue.

"Hey," Abe said to get Dot's attention. "Are you okay? You're not moving. At all. Are you even breathing?"

"I guess it's not porn. But I do love it. And I think I could do better. Can we do this? And why is it all women being tortured?"

DOT'S ATTEMPT TO HURT A MAN

"Madam has a whole segment for people who get creative. Those that we saw today were chopped up to be short because they were generic. The type of stuff you can see in any movie or read about in any book. The good parts hadn't even started yet. That was more like an intro," Abe explained. "I must say, I like how you think, honey. It's no wonder why I love you so much."

Both Abe and Dot were masked, and also wearing gloves, and dressed in all black. Even naked Jeff now had a potato sack over his head. It would allow him to breathe, but not be recognizable.

Dot was aware of where she stood, and tried her best to keep the majority of her body off camera, and Abe zoomed the lens in on Jeff's flaccid penis that was resting in the crevice of his hip.

"Should I talk?" Dot asked.

"If you want. I can change all of that later before we send it in to the show. Use some kind of voice synthesizer or something artificially created."

Dot held up what she was holding. "This is a hair straightener. Something most of us gals with curly hair have used at some point or another."

She held it up, demonstrating how it was similar to a pair of pliers. You grip the handle, squeeze, and that brings the ceramic plates together, which was designed to hold hair and essentially iron until it's straight.

"This has been plugged in for over fifteen minutes. These plates are hot," she explained. "This specific straightener is designed for thick, stubborn hair. If you can believe what the packaging says, these ceramic plates heat up to over four hundred degrees Fahrenheit."

Abe couldn't help but laugh in anticipation.

"Let's see what we can do with this floppy dick."

Upon Dot's touch, Jeff's cock jerked, some form of an involuntary spasm; a reaction to sudden stimuli. Even without being full of blood, his penis was thick and wide with girth. Short, but kind of stumpy. If engorged, no telling how large it would become.

Carefully, as to not burn herself, Dot used one hand on the straightener, the other on his shaft to place it between the two piping-hot ceramic plates.

The instant that the top side of his stick hit the heat, his bare flesh only lightly touching the fever of the hair tool, his cock tried to jump away to find relief.

Only to find that where it had jumped towards was equally hot and painful.

Dot laughed wickedly as she squeezed her hand, closing the improvised weapon, two sides of scorching pain coming together to wreak havoc and agony to his most delicate body part.

Jeff's body tensed, his thigh muscles practically building out of his skin, trying to free his body from his restraints.

Skin sizzled.

Steam rose into the air.

The harder Dot squeezed, the more his shaft thinned, adopting its forced shape, and rolls of meat squished out from between the hot plates.

Even the tip of his pecker, a portion of meat that wasn't directly affected by the heat, turned red and then purple, swelled with torment.

Abe was not laughing. He couldn't help but to turn his head and look away, sympathetic for his girlfriend's prisoner. Having owned a penis himself meant that he could almost feel the pain as much as if it was being inflicted to him.

"How long should I hold it like this?" Dot asked, her nose so close that she could smell an indecipherable aroma. Nothing like she'd ever smelled before. "When I straighten my hair, it only takes seconds. But this is different, right?"

Abe looked up, only to see that he must had muted his ears temporarily, because he never heard Jeff's sounds; a cross between the howl of a wounded animal and also the muscles of his esophagus working backwards, bringing anything that had been in his stomach regurgitating under the sack mask.

The improvised mask moistened, smells of burning flesh floating through the air now meshed with the raunchy stench of stomach bile.

"I'll do just as I do with my hair!" Dot exclaimed in excitement.

Still squeezing the straightening iron, she pulled Jeff's pecker away from his body, same as she would do with her curls, gliding the iron down her hair and away from her scalp.

As the hair straightener moved away, the nest-like mound of Jeff's pubic hair was revealed to be singed.

It was a slow process, taking almost two full minutes at glacial speed to cover the entirety of the few inches of penis.

A LITTLE BIT OF DAMAGE

It was hard for Abe to look.

His mind was torn whether he was sympathetic or empathetic to Jeff's wound, but it made no difference. Seeing Dot this happy was all that mattered to him.

Abe forced a smile.

Dot leaned in close to get an up close view of the havoc she had wreaked on Jeff's sex organ. "Do you think this qualifies as a third degree burn?"

Abe shrugged and forced himself to look. "Is there a such as a fourth degree burn?"

The cock was now flatter, the girth flattened and exchanged for a small portion of length.

The squared ceramic plates left behind instant blisters, and burnt flesh.

Abe even noticed that some of the flesh was still sizzling on the hot weapon. Meaning that flesh had been fully removed, lifted away from Jeff's body to forever burn away into a steam of nothingness.

The colors of the penis, swift changes and mixtures of reds, pinks, purples, browns, blacks and even white (which was presumably fluid leaking from the large burst blisters).

It no longer resembled a piece of male anatomy.

It was just a leaking lump of meat, scorched and ruined, perched atop crispy pubic hair.

"How'd I do?" Dot asked. "Think I'll make it on that vagina show?"

Abe shrugged.

"You don't know? Seriously? It's much funner than those weak videos we watched a few minutes ago. Do you think that you could do better?"

Abe shrugged, smiled, and accepted the challenge.

ABE'S ATTEMPT TO HURT A WOMAN

The smells of bleach and gasoline danced in the air, a foul corruption of clean versus nasty substance, tangling like one odor was fighting to overtake the other.

Abe's nose blindness didn't think much of it, but Dot's olfactory senses worked overtime trying to decipher between the contrast.

Jen, her head also covered, her mouth gagged, and nude, tied down to another table, cried and screamed as best she could. It was highly likely that she could also smell the strange aroma through the fabric, and possibly her tortured mind couldn't make sense of it either.

Two mason jars, one clearly labeled with sloppy handwriting 'BLEACH' the other jar labeled 'GAS', for the sake of the camera.

"I don't have a front cavity, but I do have an ass," Abe spoke aloud. "I think the gas would be worst."

Dot watched with amusement and didn't respond.

If it weren't for Dot and her bag, Abe wouldn't have access to tampons. His thought, while brainstorming ideas, was to use simple cotton balls. It was his lovely girlfriend that offered him the idea of using tampons instead.

A product designed to absorb as much fluid as possible, and then easy to navigate into tight holes.

"My fingers are calloused so they don't hurt to touch. Can you explain again why you'd think it hurt inside of her?" Abe asked.

"I don't know, Abe. Call it intuition. I learned in college that girls would soak their tampons in vodka, and shove them up inside themselves to get drunk quicker."

"What? Are you sure? Is that a real thing? Is that even safe? Or were they just pranking you?"

"I don't know. Something about mucous membrane and capillaries and sensitivity. Suppose you'll never know until you try it."

Jen must have heard the conversation, because she screamed louder through her gagged mouth, her voice rising from somewhere deep inside out of pure fear. That made Dot laugh.

"Well, it seems pretty boring to me," Abe spoke from a place of honesty. "Can we do something beforehand, something that would really hurt before we stick soaked tampons up in her?"

"Like what?"

Abe shrugged. "I don't know. Cut up in there first? That would make a good video, but would also ensure that the bleach and gas would really really really hurt. Imagine scraping your knee, and cleaning it out with bleach. That would be painful."

"Sure."

+++++

"What's that?" Dot asked.

"It's a file. It's like sandpaper, but metal, much more durable, and has a handle similar to a handle of a screwdriver. Easy to hold and use."

Poised so that the camera had a clear view, Abe held the tool, and he leaned in between Jen's spread legs. "This is like prep."

"Does that turn you on?"

Abe shrugged. "Not her anatomy, no. But the thought of what I'm fixing to do? Yes. For sure."

The camera was mounted, so Dot's only job was to observe. "You sure you don't want me to zoom in or anything?"

"I'll do that after I do this."

The long sliver of metal, at least a foot in length, and a little over an inch wide, slid into Jen's dry vagina with force. The tied-up woman's abdominal muscles flinched in response, out of the sense of being invaded.

Similar to one using a dildo or another type of sex toy, Abe began gyrating his arm, back and forth, pressing the file deeper into Jen's vagina and then pulling it back close to him.

Other than Jen screaming, it was silent. It wasn't like sanding wood, no sound to accompany the smoothness, but there was blood dripping from her small cavity as her vaginal walls were being sloughed away, to uncover more tender, more sensitive layers of female innards.

SELF TESTS

Abe was now behind the camera, zooming in on the damage he had caused. Well, he was zooming in on what could be seen. Due to the injuries being technically up inside of Jen, and out of sight, there was only inflamed flesh and blood that he was filming.

"Yeah, super boring. Nowhere near as good as my video," Dot boasted.

"But look. At the entry of her butthole, it's like the worst carpet burn ever. I literally sanded away her skin. Imagine what it looks like up inside there. Even her pussy lips are swollen and bleeding. There has to be a ton of damage up in there."

"Yeah. You think? Then show me?"

Abe scratched his head. "How do you make a butthole wider? Or should I try with her female pocket first? Isn't that easier to stretch? Like, when women have babies, doesn't it get really big?"

"It does get big, but it also tears."

"Does that mean I could cut it open? For example, if I were to snip that meaty wall that separates her front and back sides? Would we be able to see up in there? With maybe a flashlight or something?"

This was a time for Dot to now shrug.

"Okay. I'll do the tampons first. Then we'll cut it open."

++++

Just to test his pain theory, Abe used the file to sand away a tiny patch of flesh on the backside of his hand. Skin rolled beneath the textured metal file until it eroded away.

Through gritted teeth, Abe stopped, unable to willingly inflict any more pain to himself. "Think that's good enough?"

"It's pink. What am I seeing under there? Muscle?"

Abe shrugged. "I don't know. Take the eyedropper and do it."

Dot chose the bleach first, plunged the eyedropper into the mason jar, and then sprinkled a few dots onto Abe's patch of broken skin on the back of his hand.

"Shit!" he screamed, and immediately jerked his hand away from her. After shaking it several times, he ran to the bathroom sink to try and wash away the offending substance. "This hurts!"

Dot was so tickled that she couldn't stop laughing. "Man up! It can't hurt that bad!"

"Want to bet?" Abe asked.

Dot shook her head to signify 'no'. "C'mon. Get back in here. Let's try the gas."

"Naw. I'm good. I'm sure it'll hurt."

"Whatever. Okay."

It was silent for a few moments as Abe dried the water and patted his injury gently, and blew on it for some reason. "My mom used to do this. When I was a kid, whenever I was hurt. She'd kiss my boo-boos, and blow on them."

"Blow on it? Did that work?"

"I don't know. Possibly. Made me feel better overall. There's nothing like mommy medicine to get the job done."

"Are you going to get all sappy on me now? Like you did when you told that story about your mom and that stick with the nail in it? Why'd you never tell me about that before?"

Abe shrugged. "I don't know. I guess because I haven't told you everything. I will in time, maybe. You want me to tell you now?"

"Nope. We have more fun things to attend to. Such as shoving these tampons up that girl and cutting her open so that we can see up inside of her. And, by the way, my video is much more entertaining than yours. I'm sure I'll make it on that vagina show before you will."

Abe shrugged.

FUNNY TAMPONS

"Gas in the ass? Bleach in the peach?" Abe asked. "How that's sound? I think I should do the gas first."

With a tampon in hand, it dripping with stenchy gasoline, Dot was giving Abe a crash course on how to insert it. "Put the plastic applicator inside the desired hole, then push the other end, like it's a needle or something. Just push, and let it glide up inside her."

The blood trailing out of Jen's rectum had now dried up, but the moisture off the tampon applicator re-wetted it, making it look sticky.

A portion of the cotton part of the tampon overflowed from the tip of the applicator, due to it being wet and having absorbed so much gasoline, changing its shape.

It wasn't easy fitting the item into the tight anus, and Dot even had to help spread Jen's butt cheeks.

"This is such a boring video," Dot said loudly. "Not good at all."

Which almost angered Abe. It gave him the determination to make this work. No matter how hard he pushed, the tampon wouldn't slide inside of her.

"You're pushing too hard," Dot instructed.

"Whatever." Outdone with the whole situation, Abe threw the tampon to the side, and picked up the eyedropper. "This is bound to work."

The dropper was smaller than the tampon, now full of gas, and slid easily into Jen's backside. Abe squeezed the bulb, releasing the toxic fluid inside her sanded out rectum.

Jen's body tensed, shifted. She cried through her gag. It obviously hurt, but Dot thought it was almost boring to watch. There was no obvious damage to view.

"Now the bleach in the peach," Abe said, filling the eyedropper with bleach, inserting it into her vagina, and releasing the liquid into the cavity where the vaginal walls had been rubbed away.

"Still boring," Dot commented.

"I'll show you boring."

Abe's words didn't make sense.

PART FIVE: START OF END

DGAF

Abe pulled a lighter from his pocket and flicked it, the flame dancing.

"Abe? What are you doing?"

He never answered Dot's question.

Instead, he poured the rest of the gasoline on Jen's body and set it on fire. The liquid mingled with the flame, Jen's flesh being the first to burn.

The stench was out of this world, but the change of her pale skin to a dark crispy was beautiful and mesmerizing. Dot didn't want to look away, amazed by how quick fire beat skin, amazed by how hot it was from standing too close.

"It's beautiful!" Dot pointed. "Look! If you look close enough, you can see her blood boiling."

"Grab your stuff. We have to get out of here. Now!" Abe ordered.

WORLDLY BELONGINGS AND BYEBYES

Dot was glad all of her belongings were still packed away nicely in bags from her jaunt to college.

Abe wanted nothing from his home, other than his laptop computer and his camera.

They grabbed what they wanted and rushed out the door.

"Was that boring?" he asked.

Dot nodded. "Unexpected. And stupid. But not boring."

Standing in the distance, they stood and watched as the home was now burning higher and wider than any bonfire party they'd ever attended.

"Guess that's it for Jen and Jeff?" Abe asked.

Dot shook her head. "Where to now?"

"I have a couple of things to tend to here. Let's put this stuff in the truck first."

++++++

Abe walked fast, and with a purpose, leading Dot.

"Think we can load a cow in the back of the truck?" Abe asked. "She's my friend."

"Like lift a cow? Doubt it."

"I'm funning with you," Abe laughed. "I have a trailer for her. I'll hook it to the truck. There's something else I want to show you."

Dot didn't ask any questions, even though a lot of them were running through her mind. *What would they do with a cow? Also, how long until the police or fire trucks arrived? Could she feign that she'd been his prisoner all along? Would that clear her from the two dead bodies they're bound to find in the home?*

And last, but not least, what was so important that Abe had to show her?

"My ma, I'm sure she'd have liked you," Abe said. "My pa, not so much. He was a mean sonuva."

"Why are you going on about your parents again? Have you lost your damn mind?"

"Almost there."

++++

The silo was dark, but Dot could smell it before they entered.

The smell of death. A worse smell than Jen burning alive.

Dot paused outside the door. "Abe, how many

people have you killed? Are you keeping bodies in here? If so, we need to burn it down, too."

"I've never killed anyone," Abe confessed, "unless Jeff and Jen died in the fire."

Dot looked back at the blazing home. "They're dead. They have to be. No way they escaped. What's in here?"

"My parents. I have to say goodbye."

Dot waited outside and didn't ask any questions, all the while, her mind churning out ideas and hopes that they'd make it off the farm before the authorities showed up to contain the fire.

THE COW

"You took long enough in the silo!" Dot complained. "Now you want to load a cow in a trailer and hook it to the truck? I hear sirens. People are coming."

"I hear them, too," Abe looked off in the distance. "This won't take but maybe four minutes. Wait here."

Dot stood outside the barn, tapping her foot, speaking aloud to herself. Thinking out loud. "Should I run off? Like into the woods or something? The fire is an obvious arson. Why did he do that? He's an idiot. There's dead people in the home. And let's not forget the bodies in the silo. I'm so screwed. And a cow? He's doing this for a cow?"

Abe came speeding back in the truck, trailer in tow, Dot still standing there, spinning circles, trying to figure out which direction the sirens were blaring. "Let's get out of here!"

"We are, but I have to get Dottie first!" Abe jumped out of the truck, lowered a ramp on the trailer, and made his way inside the barn to get his bovine friend.

"Dottie? You named your cow after me?" Dot couldn't believe her ears. "You keep your dead parents in the silo, and you named a cow after me? Why? You are crazy!"

"No! I didn't name a cow after you. My dad named the cow. He loved this cow. Dottie has been my friend for many years!"

"Well, hurry it up!" Dot screamed. "I can't believe how dumb you are! First you set fire to the house, and instead of running away, you're loading up a cow?"

Abe paused for just a moment, shrugged, and continued leading Dottie into the trailer. "Chill out. It'll be okay." His words were more directed towards the cow and not his girlfriend.

++++++

Dot was waiting not so patiently in the passenger side of the truck when Abe jumped in the driver seat.

"WHY ARE YOU BEING SO DUMB? GET A MOVE ON!" she commanded.

"I'm going. I'm going." Abe pushed on the gas pedal, and steered the vehicle towards a road off the backside of the property. "It's a smaller path. The fire trucks, nor the police, know about this path back here. It's bumpy, I'll have to go slow because Dottie is in the back, but they won't catch us going this way."

Dot sighed a breath of relief.

NEXT MOVES

They drove for almost an hour, in silence, not passing a single vehicle on the rural roads. "I'm getting tired. We'll pull off soon. Being nighttime, it'll help us hide."

"Hide? Where? How?" she asked, her tone terse and full of anger.

"I have a plan. You tired? Ready to stop for the night?"

Dot didn't answer, and instead waited, after exhaling a too loud sigh.

+++++

Abe pulled off a side road, which led to a gravel road, which led to a dirt path, and a boundary of trees up ahead. "I still have Jen and Jeff's camping stuff. Tent. Cots. Cooler. Camp stove. I packed up their stuff. Looks like it'll come in handy here."

"Why?"

"We can set up camp back here. It's completely

private. Get some sleep. Even let Dottie graze. My dad used to take me hunting here. There's even a pond for freshwater."

The moment the truck parked, Abe gave all of his attention to Dot. "It's so peaceful back here. It'll buy us some time before we figure out what to do next."

"Figure out what to do next?" Dot asked. "We're basically on the run from the law. We haven't sent that video to my dad for my ransom money. And now you want me to sleep outdoors? Like with bugs? No toilets? With a stinky cow?"

"Hey," Abe said calmly. "Dottie doesn't stink that bad. She's sick. Have some compassion. C'mon." Abe opened his door, jumped out, and turned around to see that Dot hadn't moved.

"Compassion? What about compassion for me? My boyfriend is a blooming idiot and wants to live off the land like some kind of pioneer or something?"

Abe shrugged. "It's not permanent. Just so we can catch some sleep. That way our minds are fresh. To come up with some sort of plan or something."

"We had a plan! We were going to get money from my dad and have a nice life together! But no! You had to burn the house down and ruin everything!"

"Everything's not ruined," Abe assured her. "We have each other. Isn't that enough?"

"No! It's not enough! I need a proper bed! A shower and toilet! Electricity! And I need to not be near that stinking cow!"

Abe slowly climbed back into the truck, and hung his head. "A hotel? How about that? I guess it wouldn't kill Dottie to sleep in the trailer for one night in a parking lot. How's that sound?"

"It's a start. Think we can find a cheap place that takes cash and won't ask for identification?"

Abe shrugged and drove. "At least we're together."

Dot didn't respond.

As the truck picked up speed, Dottie moo'ed so loud that they could hear her from the trailer.

MOTEL CHANCES

"It's way too dim in here. That bath tub has a black ring of dirt. The toilet is stained. The mattress is too soft. The sheets need to be washed-"

Abe tuned out Dot's constant complaining and flicked on the television to distract his thoughts of Dottie, a cow forced to sleep in a trailer all night.

"Abe! Are you hearing me?"

Abe shrugged. "I hear you, babe. All that matters is that we're together, right? We have each other. There are some clean sheets in the camping supplies out in the truck. This place took cash, and didn't ask to see ID. We're safe here."

"Safe? Sure. Maybe. But dirty. And still poor. Like poorer than before, if you can believe that. You brought the camera and your computer, right? Shouldn't we be working on getting that video edited and sent to my dad? It's our last chance for getting some money."

Abe shrugged. "I'm tired. Can't we do that in the morning?"

"In the morning?" Dot shrieked. "You can't be serious? This place doesn't bother you? We need cash. Now. Like as soon as possible!"

Abe patted the empty bed beside him. "C'mere. Lie with me for a minute. Let's take a breather and just enjoy life, together. Tomorrow, I promise. We'll get everything set up. Everything will be fine."

"Whatever," Dot said, rolling her eyes backwards in her head. "I guess I have to be the one to go get the clean sheets and make the bed? Meaning I have to go out by the stinking trailer. I bet the sheets smell like that cow, too!"

"I'll do it, in just a minute. Sit with me. Hold my hand or something?"

Dot slammed the motel door behind her as she made her way outside, mumbling under her breath. "I can't believe he's this stupid. I must be stupid, too, for trusting him."

PART SIX: FINISHED

RUDE AWAKENING

Dot woke up, her body cocooned in her clean sheet, wrapped up tighter than a burrito. No matter how hard she struggled, she couldn't free her arms or legs. "Abe! Are you in the bathroom? I've gotten tangled up or something. Can you come help me?"

Seemingly voice/sound activated, the laptop computer on the table next to the bed came to life, the screen glowing.

The screen, despite being black, was illuminated. And a voice spoke.

A voice Dot knew all too well.

It was Abe.

"I'm really sorry it had to be this way," he spoke through the speakers.

"Abe! This isn't funny! Let me out!" Dot struggled so hard against the sheet that she rolled off the edge of the bed onto the dirty carpet.

"I've learned a thing or two. Such as how to record this, and make it disappear as if it never existed. And also my father taught me a thing or two."

"ABE!!!! GET IN HERE AND HELP ME YOU IDIOT!!!" Dot wrestled as much as she could, but her arms were tucked alongside her body, her legs couldn't spread, and she couldn't see what was binding her due to the sheet enveloping her. "OKAY! JOKES OVER! HA HA!"

The voice continued through the speakers. "By now, I'm sure you've figured out that you're stuck. And when you get a visitor, you can tell them you were kidnapped and forced to do what you did. But a video of you enjoying what you did will prove otherwise. Let me explain more."

Dot looked around, and realized she was alone. This was really happening.

"I loved you, Dot. I really did. But my parents taught me a thing or two. I've tried - tried hard- to explain that to you. My father wasn't always the way he turned out. According to him, a life with my mother. Her constant complaining, bitching, pestering and belittling him. Well, it changed him and made him who he was. He taught me that.

"I'm not making excuses for him. He did smack her around sometimes, but he says he wasn't always that way. I might have inherited my love for drink from him, but I never wanted to become him. He even warned me about women, how they can change a man.

"I knew all along that you were twisted like me. Especially since you were the one who came up with the idea to fake torture you to get money from your dad. And I loved that about you.

"Hell, when I kept you tied up with Jeff and Jen, I did that for your own protection. And what'd you do? Get competitive. Called me an idiot

"But then I realized my dad was right. Women want to change men. You wanted to change me. Calling me stupid. We had a chance to be together, but you wanted money. You wanted me to be your slave and do every little thing your way.

"My dad's demise was him drunk, waving a gun around, mom beating him with that stick with the nail. Until she grabbed a knife and stabbed him. Him shooting her. Them both dead. I always feared that stick, but I feared dad's warning about loving a woman even worst.

"I don't want to end up like them, so here we are. This recording will disappear. Every video of me has disappeared. But every evil thing you did on the camera, will play on a loop. Evidence of the bitch that you truly are.

"As for me, I have Dottie. Will live off the land, remembering the good times with you. Yeah, maybe you're right. I am an idiot. But I'm an idiot with freedom."

The black screen turned into a bright white light, a video coming into focus of Dot torturing Jeff.

Dot cried.

Minutes later, there was a knock on the motel room door. "Police! We have the place surrounded! Come out with your hands up!"

Dot knew it was over.

At any moment, the police would come into the room and see the video of her with a smile on her face taking a hair straightener to Jeff's dick.

A BOY AND HIS COW

Abe watched his bobber floating in the water, fishing pole in hand, and a small tear flowing down his cheek.

"This does hurt, being without her," he said to his cow, whose head was cocked sideways, studying him. "But it's for the best, right? I love her, but she didn't appreciate that. At least my parents taught me some real life lessons. Could I ever truly trust her? No. At least I didn't kill her. She'll be fine in prison, or maybe she'll get lucky and get sent to some mental institution. I don't have to watch over my shoulder, afraid she might come kill me."

His bobber went under the water, Abe jerked on his pole and set the hook, reeling in a catfish.

"See, life's still good." Abe smiled at his bovine friend. "Dot wasn't nice. She didn't even like you, and you're my true friend. Think you can make it across the border with me? Mexico is a few hours drive, but once we get there, I'll find you a pond and some fresh grass."

A NOTE FROM THE DARK MIND OF SEA CAUMMISAR

The Light and the Stick
The Stick and the Light
Strange title for a story, huh? I agree.

Is there some symbolism buried there? Maybe. Maybe not. If you think hard enough, there probably is. If you don't want to think about that and just enjoy the story, that's fine too. There's no right or wrong way to read something. (unless maybe you read something you're not enjoying. Life's too short to spend time doing stuff you don't enjoy...)

It's a personal experience for everyone.

My own mother came up with that title. Even posed for the cover photo. And helped me with the ideas.

Not that this will mean anything to you as a reader,

but every night in my home, we take the two pups out the back sliding patio door, and we turn out the light and place a stick in the track of the door (just an added precaution to also locking the sliding patio door).

My mother, who lives with me and hubby, would say 'I have the light and the stick' when I'd bring the dogs inside from the last daily potty. She'd turn out the light, lock the door, and place the stick.

I heard that phrase so much and even laughed about it, that mom said I should write a book about it… she said it multiple times… and I put off some of my projects to work on this idea with her.

Not to get too real here, but mom was diagnosed a few months back with small cell lung cancer. Her diagnosis happened at about the same time I lost my father to lung cancer (I hate the phrase 'lost' he's not lost. Just no longer in this world).

Anyway, that's where this idea stems. Which means nothing to the readers, but for me personally, maybe I can see some symbolism, something deeper in the title.

It's fine if you don't.

As far as the story, Abe seemed to learn many things from his parents.

Fear. Can fear be taught? Or is it instinct?

Maybe it depends on context.

Maybe it means something.

Maybe it means nothing.

Abe shrugged often in this book…. I wanted it to

demonstrate how laid back and easy going he was at the root of his character...

If this had been a romance story, maybe love would have prevailed.

But this isn't romance. It's extreme horror. Love lost. Fear won. Deep-instilled fears of who Abe was, or who he may have become as a person. How's that for personal growth?

For the record, I hate the word 'idiot', but feel like it fit Dot's constant complaining. Felt like an appropriate word from a character like her.

And who noticed the 'My Vagina Smells Like Sulfur' easter egg? It was hidden in plain sight. Another way to demonstrate Abe and Dot's curiosity of the dark side, Dot's jealousy of Madam Midnite, etc......

I also hate writing gun scenes (Dot shooting Jeff). Guns are anticlimactic. Too quick. Too easy.

... I actually dreamt I was shot the night I wrote that scene..

Maybe I'm thinking too hard about stuff.

If I were a reader, I'd have just read the story and not put a lot of thought into it. Which is what I expect most people would do.

At the very least, I hope you found the story entertaining....

Good thing it's fiction..... Nothing here to psychoanalyze. My only hope is that it entertained you. If so, I consider my job done. If I didn't entertain you, so very sorry.

If you liked this story, I have plenty of other titles available to read…

Stay dark my friends.
Until next time.

If you're like me and don't spend much time on social media, here's a good old fashioned email. sharoncheatham81@gmail.com. Do you have any questions, comments, complaints, or compliments? I'd love to hear from you.

I read often and love Goodreads, too. If you want to keep up with what I'm reading, I'm Sea Caummisar on Goodreads.

Until then, Stay Dark My Friends,
See ya next read,
Your Friend,
Sea Caummisar

Contact Info for Sea Caummisar
Facebook (Sea Caummisar)
Twitter (@seacaummisar)
Goodreads (Sea Caummisar)

Printed in Great Britain
by Amazon